Please Return to:
Sarah Brady
G. Mayne

D0531948

THE BOY WHO DREAMED
OF AN ACORN

by LEIGH CASLER

ILLUSTRATED by SHONTO BEGAY

PHILOMEL BOOKS   NEW YORK

The Boy Who Dreamed of an Acorn is an original work of fiction based upon a Native American rite known as the spirit quest. Although this particular story is set in the Pacific Northwest, various forms of the spirit quest have been practiced in Native American cultures from coast to coast.

Chinook jargon is a special common language that was once used by many tribes in parts of Oregon and the Northwest. Some Chinook words are still in use today. Following is a list of words from this story and their Chinook spelling and pronunciation.

acorn	*kahnaway*	kä' nă wā
black bear	*itchwoot*	ĭtc'h wot
blackbird	*klale tenas kalakala*	klāl / tĕn' äs / kä lăk' ä lä
camas	*kamass*	käm' äs
eagle	*chakchak*	chäk' chäk
earth	*illahee*	ĭl' lä hē
elk	*moolock*	moo' lŭk
fire	*piah*	pĭ ä
fox	*hyas opoots talapus*	hĭ ăs' / ō' pōōts / talapus
grizzly	*siam itchwoot*	sĭ am / ĭtc'h woot
hawk	*shakshak*	shäk' shäk
huckleberries	*shot olallie*	shot / ō lä' lĭ
mountain	*stone illahee*	stone / ĭl' lä hē
mountain lion	*hyas pish pish*	hĭ ăs' / pĭsh / pĭsh
mouse	*hoolhool*	hol hol
oak tree	*kull stick*	kŭl / stick
sky	*koosagh*	kōō' sä
willow tree	*eena stick*	ē' nä / stick
wolf	*leloo*	le loo

The author wishes to express her gratitude to Selene Rilatos-Lynch, tribal historian of the Confederated Tribes of the Siletz Indians, for her assistance and her support.

Text copyright © 1994 by Leigh Casler. Illustrations copyright © 1994 by Shonto Begay. All rights reserved. This book, or parts thereof, may not be reproduced in any form without permission in writing from the publisher. Philomel Books, a division of The Putnam & Grosset Group, 200 Madison Avenue, New York, NY 10016. Published simultaneously in Canada. Printed in Hong Kong by South China Printing Co. (1988) Ltd. Text design by Patrick Collins. The text is set in Aldus.

Library of Congress Cataloging-in-Publication Data   Casler, Leigh. The boy who dreamed of an acorn/Leigh Casler. p. cm. Summary: At first disappointed that his mountain quest has only given him a dream of a tiny acorn, a young boy comes to recognize that his position in his tribe is as strong as the tree that grows from the acorn. 1. Chinook Indians—Juvenile fiction. [1. Chinook Indians—Fiction. 2. Indians of North America—Fiction. 3. Dreams—Fiction. 4. Self-perception—Fiction.] I. Title. PZ7.C26824Bo 1994 [E]—dc20 92-44902 CIP AC
1 3 5 7 9 10 8 6 4 2
First Impression

For my parents, who taught me to love the earth.
And for my teachers, who taught me to love words.

—L.C.

For all past, present, and future students
of Shonto Boarding School,
and to all Navajo children everywhere.

—S.B.

On a night when thin white clouds passed slowly in front of a fat yellow moon, three young boys made their way in silence to the slopes of a great mountain. Others before them had come to this mountain, and others had climbed its slopes in silence. And all who came to make this climb came searching for a dream.

Like the others who had come to the mountain before them, the three boys hoped to dream a dream of power: to dream of the mountain lion, or the grizzly, or the wolf. Any of these would bring many lessons to the dreamer. Any of these would bring him strength and skill. And so, as the boys made their way up the mountain, they hoped for such a dream.

A short way up from the foothills, one boy stopped. Here, where the water sang to him, he chose to stay. So here he built his fire and stared into its flames until sleep came to him and his eyes closed. And when he dreamed, he dreamed of a huge black bear sitting by a river. And when he awoke, he knew that he would learn many things in his lifetime from the bear.

Farther up the mountainside, the second boy stopped. Here, where the stars danced for him, he chose to stay. So here he built his fire and watched its flames until sleep came over him and his eyes closed. And when he dreamed, he dreamed of a white-headed eagle flying through the sky. And when he awoke, he knew that in his lifetime the eagle would teach him many things.

The third boy did not stop until he had reached the very top of the mountain. Here there was no water to sing to him, and here the stars did not dance. But the boy had heard it said that the highest places often brought the strongest dreams. So here, where the wind howled and the dust flew, he chose to stay.

The boy was tired and hungry from his climb, but he did not eat or rest. He built his fire as the others had, and he looked long into its flames before sleep overcame him and his eyes closed. And when he dreamed, he dreamed only of a small brown acorn lying in a shady grove. And when he awoke, he knew only that the dream he had hoped for had not come. For what kind of power could there be in an acorn? What was its strength or skill? It could not help him hunt or fish. It could not make him swift or strong. What lessons could it teach him?

All these questions the boy kept to himself, until he went to see the wisest man in his village. Before this man the boy sat, and to this man only did he speak of his dream. "To the top of the mountain I climbed," he told the wise man. "High above the place where the huckleberries grow. There I built my fire and hoped to dream a dream of great power.

"But I did not dream of the mountain lion, or the grizzly, or the wolf. Not one of them came to me. Not even the squirrel or the blackbird came. Instead, I dreamed of a thing without feet or wings, without teeth or claws—a thing so small it can be held in one hand. Tell me, what does such a dream mean?"

And the wise man said to him:

"To each a different gift is given,
and to each a different dream does come.
To one comes the eagle, to one comes the bear.
To one comes the elk or the fox.
The owl and the field mouse—each has its power.
The hawk and the weasel—each is a teacher.
Each has a gift it can share."

"Are these words true?" the boy asked. "Even for an acorn?"
The wise man nodded. "Even for an acorn they are true. So I say to you:

Be happy with your own gift,
and be at peace with your own dream.
For in the smallest of acorns there is a thing that is mighty,
and the seasons will show you the wonders it holds."

Then, slowly, the wise man opened a worn leather pouch he had at his side. From it he brought forth a single shining acorn. This he placed in the boy's hands, saying, "Go now, and plant this. Grow as it grows."

And this the boy did. Into the earth he put the acorn, and then he watched with wonder.

He saw the acorn struggle as it pushed its way out of the ground, and he saw the first of its branches and leaves appear. He gave it water when days were dry, and when winds blew hard, he gave it a stick to lean upon. Some nights, when no one was listening, he sang songs to the little tree.

For many seasons the boy did these things. And he did other things, too. With his father and his elders he went to fish along the river, and with his uncles and his cousins he went hunting in the woods. He was not old enough, yet, to go without others. But soon he would be able to do these things alone.

Three times the first blue flowers of the camas arrived, and three times the dark red fruits of the chokecherry ripened. Three times the stalks of the wapatoo turned brown and dry, and three times the wands of the willow stood bare and white—white with the first snows of winter.

For all these seasons the boy was at peace with his dream. He was happy just to care for the tree and to grow as it grew. He was happy until the day he heard the people of his village talking about the boy who had dreamed of the bear.

"See how strong he is!" he heard the people say. "See how many fish he has caught, and how many he can carry! Like a bear he fishes. Like a bear, using only his hands!"

And the people were glad that the boy who had dreamed of the bear lived among them. But the boy who had dreamed of the acorn was sad at heart when he heard their words. For he could not catch many fish, and he could not carry heavy loads.

Now, when the boy cared for the young tree, he was no longer happy. And though he watered it and watched over it as he had before, his heart could not see its wonders. Five times came the flowers of the camas and the fruits of the chokecherry, and five times the stalks of the wapatoo turned brown. The snows of five winters came and went—and still the boy did not see its wonders.

Then came an even darker day. The day when he heard the people speaking of the boy who had dreamed of the eagle.

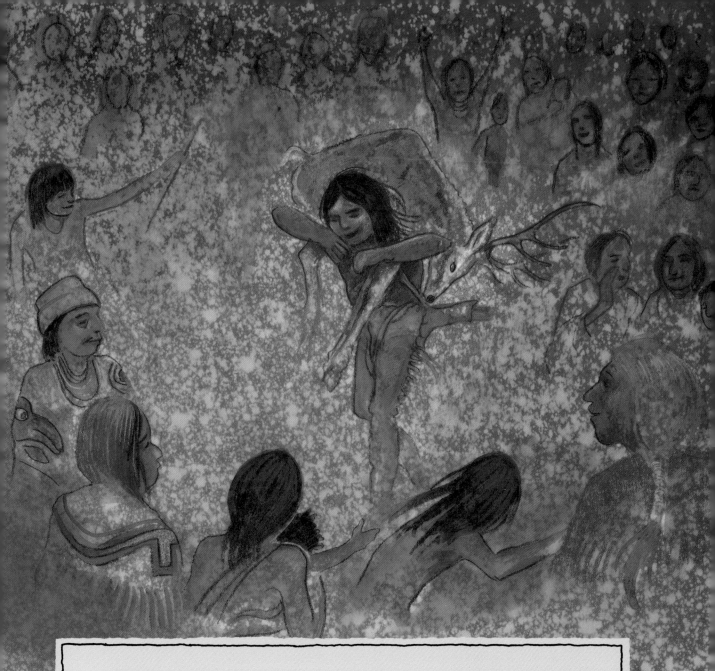

"What a hunter he is!" he heard them say. "Like an eagle who sees beyond mountains! Always he can spot a deer, and always he is first to reach it."

And the people were glad that the boy who had dreamed of the eagle lived among them. But the boy who had dreamed of the acorn was not glad. The words of his people brought more sorrow than his heart could hold. For he could not see beyond mountains, and he was never first to reach a deer.

"Why couldn't *I* have dreamed of the eagle?" he cried out to the sky. "Why couldn't *I* be strong like the bear?"

But the sky did not answer. So the boy went once again to see the wisest man in all his village. Before this man the boy sat and told of his sorrow. Like a muddy river flooding its banks, his sorrow poured out of him. And when the boy had finished his telling, the wise man said these words once more:

"To each a different gift is given,
and to each a different dream does come.
To one comes the eagle, to one comes the bear.
To one comes the elk or the fox.
The owl and the field mouse—each has its power.
The hawk and the weasel—each is a teacher.
Each has a gift it can share.
So again I say: Be happy with your own gift,
and be at peace with your own dream.
For in the smallest of acorns there is a thing that is mighty,
and the seasons will show you the wonders it holds."

Then, slowly, the wise man pulled the boy to his feet. He took the boy's hands in his own and spread his arms wide as branches, saying, "Go now, to your own gift. Stand as it stands."

And this the boy did. At the dawning of every day and the falling of every night, he stood with his arms spread wide like the branches of the tree. At first he felt very foolish standing there. Around his head the blue jays squawked, and at his feet the chipmunks scolded. And the howling wind surrounded him with clouds of flying dust. But as dawn followed night and night followed day, he began to forget to feel foolish. And he began instead to see what had become of the little tree—the tree that had grown from a single shining acorn.

Over the seasons the tree had grown, and now many creatures came to it for their shelter and their food. The squirrel came, and the blackbird, the opossum and the lark. Some days, even the bear came to feed upon its acorns. And some nights, even the eagle came to sleep among its branches. Even the people of his village came to gather at the tree. And to all who came, the tree gave freely, and for them all it made a place.

Seeing this, the boy was filled with wonder. At last he began to learn what the acorn had to teach him.

And, like the tree, he grew.

He was never given the speed of the eagle. He was never given the strength of the bear. But when his people were troubled, it was to him that they came. And when they spoke of him, they spoke with gladness, saying: "How gentle he is with the young ones! How kind he is to the old! And what he has he shares with all, for all are in his heart."

And their words were true. For the boy who had dreamed of an acorn became a man whose heart branched out wide like an oak tree, giving kindness and shelter to all who came his way. He was a man who was happy with his own gift, and at peace with his own dream.